Dingo the Mule

Palmetto Publishing Group
Charleston, SC

Dingo the Mule
Copyright © 2019 by Scott Cliver
All rights reserved

First Edition

Printed in the United States

Hardcover: 978-1-64111-537-7
Paperback: 978-164111-263-5
eBook: 978-1-64111-634-3

DiNGO
THE MULE

Who Thought He Was a Horse

Scott Cliver
illustrations by Anne Wertheim

IT WAS A BEAUTIFUL MORNING ON THE FARM.

The sun shone brightly, and something very special happened inside the barn: Two young colts were born.

They were born right next to each other and had beautiful horses as mothers who nursed them and loved them with all of their hearts.

They loved to play together as they grew up. They were best friends. They rolled, ran, and kicked up their hooves, day after day, as they played.

As they grew up together, as much as they were alike, they were different. Bongo was a horse and Dingo was a mule. Bongo's mom and dad were both horses. Dingo had a horse for a mom and a donkey for a dad. Nevertheless, both thought they were the same, but Dingo was a mule, not a horse like his best friend Bongo.

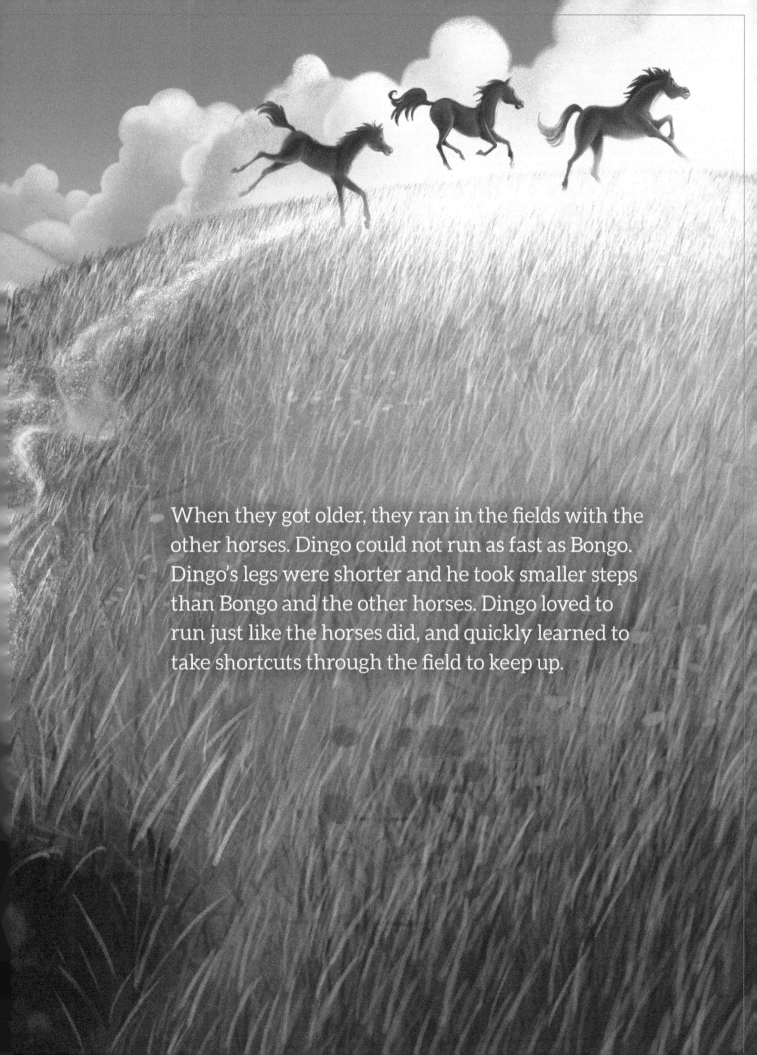

When they got older, they ran in the fields with the other horses. Dingo could not run as fast as Bongo. Dingo's legs were shorter and he took smaller steps than Bongo and the other horses. Dingo loved to run just like the horses did, and quickly learned to take shortcuts through the field to keep up.

One day after a big run, Dingo said to Bongo, "Isn't it great to be a horse? I love being a horse. I love running, jumping, and feeling the wind go past my ears and nose. I love being a horse."

As Dingo was saying how much he loved being a horse, the other horses overheard him. They all looked at each other and nodded in agreement. It was time to tell Dingo he was not a horse. They went to his best friend Bongo and said, "Since you are his best friend, we think you should be the one to tell Dingo he is not a horse."

Bongo put his head down, shaking it side to side, and said, "I cannot do this."

After a lot of nudging from the other horses, Bongo walked over to where Dingo was happily jumping and kicking around. Bongo said, "There is something I have been meaning to tell you." Dingo said, "Like what?" with a big smile. Bongo added, "It is very hard for me to say." Putting his head down, he quietly said, "You are not a horse."

Dingo said excitedly, "What are you talking about? Of course I am a horse!" Bongo said, "Let's go down to the pond and I will show you."

They went down to the pond and looked over so they could see their reflections in the water.

Bongo said, "Do you see how my ears are shorter and more pointed? Yours are much longer, bigger, and a little droopy. Look how long your face is and how much shorter mine is. My legs are longer; yours are shorter. Your eyes are different, and so are your teeth."

Bongo added, "Can you do this?" He took a very deep breath and let out an incredible whinny, with a major lip vibration at the very end. Then Dingo took a deep breath and let out a squeaky, loud *honnnk*. All of the barnyard animals laughed hysterically at the sound. Dingo and Bongo stood there for a moment. Bongo could see that Dingo was getting very sad. Then Bongo said, "There is some good news. You are half horse and you are half . . . you are half . . . you are half donkey."

Dingo started to realize he was different as he stared at his reflection in the water. Dingo's big ears went down. His head went down. His eyes became very sad as he realized for the first time that he was not a horse.

Dingo slowly turned and started walking. He was very confused, and wondered, *Who am I?*

He walked past the ducks, past the the barn, the pigs, and the chickens. Dingo kept walking down the driveway toward the road. He took one last look back at the farm and he could see the other horses running in the field. He lifted his head slightly, but it quickly went back down. As he continued to think, Dingo just kept walking and walking down the road, and for hours, he just kept walking. Night came, the wind started blowing, and it began to rain. It started thundering, and lightning was striking all around. Dingo was suddenly very, very scared.

Dingo started to shiver. Dingo realized he was in trouble. Then suddenly a stranger appeared in the middle of the road. He said, "Follow me. I have a dry, warm barn and plenty of hay for you to eat." Dingo was excited at this news. A warm, dry barn and lots of hay sounded very good.

Dingo followed the stranger to a barn. It was warm and dry, and there was plenty of hay to eat. Dingo ate until he was full, then laid down and fell into a deep sleep.

Morning came, and as Dingo stood up, he was immediately bridled with a bit in his mouth and leather straps were all over him. He had been harnessed to pull a plow. The farmer took him to the field, put Dingo in front of a plow, and cracked the whip, which scared him, and Dingo began pulling the plow.

Back at the farm, Bongo had been missing his best friend Dingo. He missed him so much, he packed his bags and set out on a journey into the sunset looking for his best friend Dingo.

Dingo pulled the plow week after week, and month after month.

Dingo grew stronger and stronger, and the plows got bigger and bigger. One day, the farmer hooked him to a new very large plow. Dingo was straining with all his might to pull this plow, with the farmer cracking his whip, when suddenly a huge plume of gas with the sound of thunder came out from under Dingo's tail.

This made the farmer very, very angry. He began choking and coughing, and began cracking the whip. Dingo jumped with all his strength and broke out of his harness. He spit out his bit, and ran as fast as he could away from the farm.

Once again, Dingo found himself walking down a road not knowing where he was going. He was cold, hungry, and scared, and thinking about his long-lost friend Bongo.

Suddenly, once again, a stranger appeared, and said to Dingo, "I have a nice warm barn and plenty of hay to eat." But Dingo was cautious. He did not want to make the same mistake as before. Then the stranger added, "I have a lot of other mules like you at my barn."

Dingo's ears went up, and he lifted his head and thought, *Wow! There are others like me!* He went home with the farmer.

The next morning, he woke up to see mules all lined up by a great big canyon. He learned people called it the Grand Canyon. The ranch hands came out and put saddles on each mule, then the people came, and each person mounted their mule for the ride down the Grand Canyon. A little boy was mounted on Dingo's back.

They talked, laughed, and enjoyed the beautiful views all the way down to the bottom of the Grand Canyon and back up. Every day, Dingo would get a new person to talk to. Dingo loved meeting new people.

Dingo loved this job, and people loved
Dingo. The trail was very narrow,
with cliffs and sharp turns. It was
very dangerous. Every once in a while
Dingo would get very close to the edge
of the cliff and kick the rocks off. His
rider would scream, and Dingo would
chuckle. Then he would say, "Don't
worry, you are safe with me."

One day, Dingo was coming out of the canyon. He heard all kinds of commotion. He saw fire trucks, ambulances, police, and all kinds of emergency vehicles. People were looking out over the edge. Dingo ran over to see what was happening. He peered over the edge. Way down, dangling from a cliff, was his terrified best friend Bongo. The firemen said, "Our ladders are too short." The rescue men said their ropes were not long enough. They did not know what to do. Dingo knew what he must do right away. Dingo yelled, "Hold on, Bongo! I am coming to get you." Fearlessly risking his life, and using his great strength and stamina, Dingo sprang into action.

Dingo went down the loose rocks, razor-sharp ledges, and tall canyon walls, and inched his way down where no one had ever been before. Dingo got to Bongo and kneeled down next to him. Dingo said, "Climb on my back and hold on tight." With all his strength, he slowly and carefully carried Bongo up to the top.

When he got to the top, he was met by a roaring, cheering crowd. Everyone was cheering. A news reporter ran up to Dingo and put a microphone in front of him. The reporter asked, "Who are you?" Dingo stood and thought, and thought some more. Dingo then slowly lifted his head high, put out his chest, and said proudly, "I am Dingo the Mule."

From that day on, they were inseparable best friends.

If you are ever driving past a horse pasture and see a horse and mule together you might be looking at Dingo and Bongo.

Let's have a Dingo Discussion

1. Describe a time when you felt different than everybody else?

   _____

   _____

   _____

   _____

2. Was there ever a time when you acted differently to fit in?

   _____

   _____

   _____

   _____

3. Did one of your friends ever tell you something that was hurtful but true? How did you deal with that?

   _____

   _____

   _____

   _____

4. Have you ever been made fun of? How did that make you feel and what did you do?

   _____

   _____

   _____

   _____

5. Have you ever seen someone that was being bullied or picked on? What could you have done to help, or how did you help?

_____

_____

_____

_____

6. Were you ever tricked into something that sounded good but turned out bad? What did you learn from that?

_____

_____

_____

_____

7. Can you think of a time where you worked hard on something you did not like, but it made you a stronger and better person?

_____

_____

_____

_____

8. When you go out of your way to do something very nice for somebody how does that make you feel?

_____

_____

_____

_____

If you want to be a hero be a best friend to somebody.

Coming Soon

DINGO MEETS DAISY

About the Author

Scott Cliver began his life in Trenton, New Jersey, and grew up in Hulmville, Pennsylvania. After serving in the U.S. Marines, he married Janie Gilbert, and together they had three sons. During this time Scott had a career as a steel worker in downtown Philadelphia for Local 401, after which he made the change to a career in construction, building and selling residences and apartments for fifteen years. In 1998 the family moved to Vail, Colorado, where he continued to build residences and commercial properties.

Scott's hobbies include skiing, snowmobiling, hunting, fishing, spending quality time with his family, and an occasional summer dip in a nearby creek.

CPSIA information can be obtained
at www.ICGtesting.com
Printed in the USA
LVHW070053121119
637081LV00019B/1255/P